Too Close to Home

Too Close to Home

Brenda Chapman

Anna Sweet Mysteries

GRASS ROOTS PRESS

First published in 2019 by Grass Roots Press

We acknowledge the financial support of the Government of Canada.

Canada

Produced with the assistance of the Government of Alberta,
Alberta Media Fund.

Government

Library and Archives Canada Cataloguing in Publication

Title: Too close to home / Brenda Chapman.
Names: Chapman, Brenda, 1955- author.
Series: Chapman, Brenda, 1955- Anna Sweet mysteries.
Description: Series statement: Anna Sweet mysteries
Identifiers: Canadiana 20190100753 | ISBN 9781771532433 (softcover)
Classification: LCC PS8605.H36 T66 2019 | DDC C813/.6—dc23

For Ted

I'd been sitting on the park bench outside the Westboro liquor store for over an hour.

Waiting.

The September sun was warm on my face. Three men had come along and asked me out for a date—a stakeout record.

"Where are you, Max Keane?" I mumbled as I scanned up and down the street. He should have been here by now.

"Hey, Anna."

I turned my head to look over my shoulder. Max stood behind me, shuffling from foot to foot. He'd snuck up on me through the back parking lot. The sight of his shy smile eased the worry in my belly.

"Hey, Max. Something hold you up?" I stood and faced him. "I expected you an hour ago."

"A guy stole my shoes and it took me a while to walk here."

I looked down at his bare, muddy feet and frayed jeans. I knew better than to show my dismay. "I guess we should go shopping then," I said in my forced, cheery voice.

"You don't need to do that."

We started walking. I was herding him toward the second-hand store further down Wellington Street. We passed a grocery store, a gas station and a couple of restaurants. Several people were out walking or biking along the busy road, enjoying the sunshine. Car traffic was steady as usual.

"Where did you sleep last night?" I asked, glancing sideways at his face.

"Found a spot in the woods off the Ottawa Parkway. I hid my sleeping bag under some bushes so all's good."

"Except for your shoes."

He grinned. "Except for my shoes."

He waited outside the store while I went inside. I knew any new clothes would make him a target for other desperate people. So I picked out a second-hand sweatshirt, jeans and running shoes in what looked like his size. I threw in warm socks and a ball cap. Fall was coming and he was going to need warmer clothes. I had to go carefully, though. He was already beginning to question my deep interest in his well-being.

He took the bag from me with a quiet thank you, and we continued down the street. We stopped at a coffee shop. Max headed for the washroom while I lined up at the counter. I was sitting at a table with sandwiches and coffee when he returned fifteen minutes later. He was wearing the new clothes and his face was free of dirt. He'd become an expert at washing up in bathroom sinks—even his hair was damp. He needed a haircut but I'd wait another week or two before offering. Most seventeen-year-old boys could get away with the shaggy look anyhow.

He held up a foot. "Shoes fit," he said. "You should be a personal shopper instead of a social worker."

So I might have lied to him about my line of work. "Not many people have my fashion sense," I agreed with a sideways smile, looking down at my wrinkled T-shirt and jeans.

When we parted outside on the sidewalk, I handed him a bag with another sandwich and a bottle of water. "See you in two days," I said. "Same time, same place."

"Yeah. See you then."

I watched Max walk away from me until he rounded the corner. I thought about following him but didn't want to risk the trust we'd taken this long to form. He was a troubled runaway and his aunt Sheila had warned me to go slowly. The family was scared he'd disappear forever if he knew they'd hired my PI firm, Storm Investigations, to watch over him. Sheila also warned me that his parents were even more scared that he'd try to take his own life . . . again.

· · · · · · · · · ·

I climbed the stairs to our office above Gino Roma's takeout pizza shop in Hintonburg. My partner, Jada Price, was talking on the phone when I entered our two-room space. She waved me over. "Here she is now," Jada said into the phone before handing it to me.

The woman's voice at the other end brought back memories. "Anna, I don't know if you remember me. I'm Gail Miller . . . from grade school."

I pictured a tall twelve-year-old with curly red hair and round glasses. "Gail. It's been a long time. How are you?"

"Good. I'm living in New Zealand. Married with three kids, so very busy."

"That's great."

"Yeah. I hear you're living with your dad and working as a private investigator. Is that right?"

"It is. Do you need help with something?"

Gail's voice lost its lightness. "If you remember, I grew up with my grandmother. Wanda Miller. She still lives in Alta Vista, near your dad. But she's not answering my calls. I'm worried. I was going to catch a flight home to check on her and then thought of you."

"You want me to pay her a visit?"

"If you would." I heard the relief in her voice across the miles. "Wanda lives in the same house as when I was a kid."

"Is she living alone?"

"Well, that's the thing. A girl answers the phone when I call. She says that she's working for my grandmother. I'm having trouble believing Wanda hired somebody to live in."

"But she might have?"

Gail took her time answering. "The girl, who calls herself Tori, always says Wanda is sleeping. She won't call her to the phone. Grandma is seventy-six and was always healthy. What is she doing sleeping all hours of the day?"

"Give me your phone number, Gail, and I'll see what I can find out."

"You don't know how much this means to me."

Jada was staring at me when I ended the call. "You forgot to tell your friend Gail about our hourly rates."

I smiled. "It's not always about the money, partner. Sometimes, you have to help out a childhood friend."

Jada shook her head. "You're a soft touch, Anna Sweet." She stood and stretched. "I've spent the day working on the books and phoning clients. We sure could use Nick in the office. When is he back in town?"

Nick. Our sometimes office manager and in-demand movie actor. My travelling boyfriend.

"He's flying home on Friday." My heart was beating faster just thinking about his arrival. I hadn't seen him for a month and missed him like crazy. I added, "We're planning a family get-together Saturday afternoon. Dad's making supper. I hope you and Henry can come by."

"I'll add it to our busy calendar," said Jada. "I can squeeze it in between watching television and doing laundry. Our Saturday nights have been lame lately. Henry is going to be thrilled to take a break from doing homework and hanging out with his sister."

CHAPTER TWO

I was getting into my car to go home when I got a text from Dad.

Pick up some ice cream and milk on your way. Supper at six.

I checked my watch. Five o'clock. No time to stop at the store and drive over to Wanda Miller's before supper. I'd go home, eat, and visit her afterwards.

My eight-year-old nephew, Evan, greeted me at the door. His beagle Sammy was right behind him. Dad's house had become Evan's second home whenever his parents were working or away. "We're having tacos for supper, Aunt Anna! Did you get the ice cream?"

"Of course. Chocolate chip cookie dough. Will that do?"

Evan gave me a thumbs up and a hug before taking the bag from my hand. He ran into the kitchen with Sammy at his heels.

Dad handed a beer to me when I entered the kitchen. He returned to frying strips of steak and chicken at the stove while Evan grated cheese. "Take a seat, Anna," Dad said. "Our Mexican feast is coming right up."

"You know the way to your daughter's heart."

"Even as a kid, I could get you to behave with a good meal. You'd do anything I asked for a slice of pie."

"The sad thing is that you're right."

After we ate, Evan and Sammy went outside to play in the yard and Dad poured us each a glass of iced tea. We remained sitting at the kitchen table. I could tell that he wanted to talk something over so I resisted the urge to get in my car and check on Wanda. "Something on your mind, Dad?" I asked after we'd almost emptied our glasses. I was worried that he was going to tell me he was sick again. He'd had a cancer scare a few years back.

"Your sister—" he started, and I relaxed against the chair back with a sigh. I drained the last of my iced tea and prepared myself.

"What about Cheri?"

"She flies into Toronto this morning from Hong Kong. Business trip. Thing is, she doesn't know if she's coming to Ottawa this time. Means she won't be home for the party."

I shrugged. "Her choice."

"She's missing all our family get-togethers. What if you ask her as a special favour to me?"

"Dad—"

"I know the two of you've been fighting. But she should be home with us."

I didn't like to see Dad upset. He rarely asked me for anything. "Okay, Dad. Don't worry about it anymore. I'll see what I can do."

Dad's smile came and went quickly as it always did when he was pleased. "Evan's been missing her. Cheri needs to spend time with her son, and the rest of us. She needs to be here."

· · · · · · · · · · ·

I parked my car between a truck and a jeep across the street from Wanda Miller's house. She lived in a red brick bungalow facing the public wading pool in Alta Vista Park. Trees and bushes shielded her house from the neighbours on either side. The sun was starting to set and lights were on inside the house.

I craned my neck to see if there was any sign of life but all was still. A green Nissan was parked in the driveway and I wrote the licence plate number in my notebook. I took out my phone and snapped photos of the car and house.

Nobody left or entered during my half-hour wait. I checked my watch. Eight o'clock. The lights in the house were still on so it looked like Wanda hadn't gone to bed. I got out of my car and walked slowly up the sidewalk. I could hear the doorbell chiming inside the house as I stood on the front step. Nobody answered. I pressed the doorbell again and waited.

"They left a few days ago," called a voice from behind me.

I turned. A white-haired man with thick glasses stood leaning on a cane. He was on the sidewalk at the end of Wanda's driveway.

"Wanda Miller?" I asked.

"No. The girl and her boyfriend who were staying with Wanda. Tori and Bevan. That's Wanda's car in the driveway. Surprised she hasn't answered the door." He frowned. "Do I know you?"

Someone called from beyond the trees: "Wait for me, Dad." A woman in her fifties jogged into view and placed a hand on the old man's arm. "You almost got away from me." She looked over at me and smiled. "Are you looking for Wanda?"

"Yes. She's not answering the door."

"That's odd. She rarely goes out."

"I understand she had a couple living with her."

"She may have. With my dad to look after, I haven't been over to see her all summer. I feel bad about that."

"So, you don't know anything about them?"

"No."

"Tori and Bevan," the old man repeated. "Wanda said she was helping them out." He squinted at me. "Do I know you?"

"My name's Anna Sweet. I'm friends with Wanda's granddaughter, Gail. She asked me to check on her."

"Well, I'm Laurie and this is my dad Hal. I live a few streets over but spend the nights with Dad after Ivy, his caregiver, leaves for the day. He's gotten ... forgetful, so I'm not sure how much weight you should give what he tells you."

"Wanda's been staying inside since those people came," said Hal. He wagged a finger in front of Laurie's nose. "Time to do the dishes, young lady. Your mother will be home soon."

"Okay, Dad." Laurie turned her face and sent me a sad smile. "Mom's been gone ten years."

They started walking slowly back toward Hal's yard. I heard Laurie talking to her father in a calming voice after they'd disappeared from view.

I could have given up and gone home. But something didn't feel right. I returned to my car and took my small tool kit out of the glove compartment. It was almost dark as I walked around the house into the back yard. Wanda had a small patio with plastic lawn chairs. The grass was overgrown and the flower garden was full of weeds.

I took out my pick and worked the lock. The door opened after a few seconds and I held my breath. No alarm to bring the neighbours and police. I stepped inside the unlit hallway and pulled the door shut behind me.

CHAPTER THREE

I stood still for nearly a minute, listening. The sound of cars passing by the house was all I heard—that and a clock ticking from somewhere deeper in the house. Satisfied I was alone, I began my search. First, I checked the kitchen. The stove and counter had been recently scrubbed down. The dishes had been washed and put away in the cupboards. I opened the door under the sink. Even the garbage had been taken out.

I walked through the door into the dining room, which led into the living room. A large picture window on the far wall faced the street. A bad smell made me wrinkle my nose. I looked around but couldn't see anything that would cause the odour. I noticed that Wanda liked teak furniture and bright pillows in red and yellow. A vase of wilted pink roses stood on a glass coffee table. The room felt modern and cozy at the same time.

As I crossed the room, the smell got stronger and I began to have an uneasy feeling. I entered the front hall and stopped in my tracks. I put a hand over my mouth. It took a moment for me to absorb the horrific sight in front of me. Wanda was lying on her back, her eyes open and staring up at the ceiling. Blood had pooled on the floor around her head.

I didn't need to go any closer to know that she was dead. The awful smell let me know that she'd been dead a while.

"Oh no," I said out loud. The shock of Wanda's death was bad enough. But I had another problem. How was I going to explain that I'd broken into her house?

I backtracked through the living room and kitchen and went outside to phone 911. If I was lucky, Detective Johnny Shaw would be on vacation and not on call. All I needed was for him to show up and figure out I'd done a break and enter.

As usual, luck was not on my side.

· · · · · · · · · · ·

Shaw, nicknamed Ice Cube by his fellow officers, arrived in the second police car. My ex-brother-in-law, a.k.a. Evan's dad, Officer Jimmy Wilson, stepped out of a third car that pulled up a few seconds later. The two men met in the middle of the road and walked directly to where I was standing next to a spruce tree. Shaw's pale blue eyes seemed resigned.

"Fancy meeting you here, Sweet," he said. "Care to tell me why you were inside the house uninvited?"

"I heard someone screaming?"

"Yeah, right. And I'm America's next top model. You, however, are a bad penny that shows up everywhere there's trouble." He paused and glared at me. "Did you know her?"

Before I could answer, he held up a hand to stop me talking. "Don't tell me. I'm going inside to see the victim. You give your story to Jimmy here. I'll deal with you later."

Jimmy grinned at me after Shaw stomped off. "He hates that you keep beating us to crime scenes. How did you manage it this time?"

"Honestly? I was only checking up on my friend Gail's grandmother. I have found out that two people were living with Gail. Their names are Tori and Bevan and they took off a few days ago."

"Last names?"

"No idea."

"Thanks, Sweet. It's a great lead anyway and we'll get on it. If you have the granddaughter's address, we can drive over and let her know the sad news."

"Pack a suitcase then, because Gail lives in New Zealand."

"Then her phone number will have to do."

We started walking toward the house. Jimmy put a hand on my arm. "Best you not be around here when Shaw comes outside. I'll let you know what we find out later."

"I'd like to phone Gail after you've given her the news. She's going to be devastated."

"I'll let you know when I've made the call."

"Thanks, Jimmy."

I watched him walk away from me before I turned and headed toward my car. I'd met Wanda Miller many times as a kid. She'd been kind and loving to Gail. Taken her in when her mother died and her father started drinking. I'd lost touch with Gail and her grandma over the years. I felt a great sadness for them both now.

I was not going to stop looking until I found Wanda's killer. Johnny Shaw would just have to move over and make room for me in his investigation.

CHAPTER FOUR

Jimmy was true to his word. He let me know early the next morning that he'd told Gail about her grandmother's death. I phoned Gail after Jimmy's call and spoke with her husband, Tom. Gail was too upset to come to the phone.

"She wants you to find out what happened to Wanda. We'll pay your fee, whatever it is."

"The police are already looking," I said.

"We want you to look, too," Tom said. "We know about police workloads."

"I'll do what I can."

I hung up and called Jimmy. "Have you tracked down the couple who'd been staying with Wanda?" I asked when he picked up.

"Hello to you too, Sweet. No, we haven't figured out Tori's and Bevan's last names. I've been tied up on a shooting case called in a few hours ago. I'm about to sit in on Wanda's autopsy."

"Okay."

"You're not going to back off from this case, are you?"

"Probably not."

"I'll cover for you with Shaw if you share what you find out."

I thought about his offer. Jimmy and I had been engaged before he took up with my sister Cheri and married her instead. After they were separated, he'd tried to start up with me again. I'd turned him down and we'd been on edge with each other since.

But bottom line, I'd do whatever it took to find Wanda's killer. Even if it meant working closely with my ex-brother-in-law. "I'll check in," I said. "Let me know what you find out from the autopsy."

He was silent for a moment. "Scratching each other's backs—so to speak. I guess you deserve to get as much as you give, Sweet."

"You can print that on my tombstone, Officer Wilson."

· · · · · · · · · ·

I swung by Wanda's house on my way to the office. Police cars were in the driveway and the yard was roped off with yellow tape. I parked around the corner and doubled back on foot. I'd spoken with the neighbour on one side of the Miller house. I hoped to catch the neighbour on the other side.

The woman who answered the door was holding a baby. A hijab covered her hair and she was wearing a cable-knit sweater and jeans. Her smile disappeared after I told her why I was there.

"I felt so bad when I heard the news," she said. "As I told the police, I didn't know her. We only moved into this house a few months ago."

"Did you see the couple who were living with Wanda?"

"I saw them but didn't pay a lot of attention. They looked to be in their early twenties. White. She was skinny with brown hair. He always wore a ball cap. That's all I remember. I'm sorry."

"That's more than I had before. Thank you."

I left her and drove downtown to my office in Hintonburg. The day was warm for September, the sun happily beating down with no clouds in sight. I opened my car window all the way to enjoy the fresh air.

I parked a few blocks from our building and took my time walking along the sidewalk. Gino waved as I passed by the window of his pizza restaurant. He was talking with two men seated at the counter so I kept going and took the stairs to our second-floor office. Jada was typing at her desk. She looked up as I entered.

"Some guy has phoned for you three times this morning."

"Max?"

"No. This fellow wouldn't leave his name or give me a message to pass along. The call display showed he was calling from a gas station."

I sat down at my desk. "Of course the caller isn't Max. He believes I'm a social worker."

Jada rubbed her forehead. "His family might be overdoing it with the secrecy. Maybe Max would be happy to know they care enough about him to hire a PI."

"I haven't figured out how the family members get along yet. Max has a younger sister and a stepfather who told the mom to stop babying Max. I don't know. If my teenage son tried to kill himself, I'd baby him, too. Max's aunt Sheila is the one who hired us. The mom and Sheila are sisters."

The office phone on my desk rang and I picked up. "Storm Investigations. Anna Sweet speaking."

The man on the other end cleared his throat. He had the deep, raspy voice of a smoker. "Anna, Max is in a bit of trouble. He's in the woods on the parkway at the end of Churchill Avenue."

"Does he need an ambulance?"

"No.

"How did you get my name and number?"

"Followed you one day after you met Max. I was worried."

"What happened to—" I found myself talking to a dial tone. The man had hung up without saying goodbye.

"I gotta go," I said, jumping up and hurrying across the room. Whoever the caller was knew Max and knew I'd been hired to look after him.

"Want any help?" asked Jada as I reached the door.

"I'll text if I need you," I called over my shoulder. "I'll find out what kind of trouble Max got himself into first."

CHAPTER FIVE

The drive to Churchill Avenue took me east through a couple of neighbourhoods. I easily reached the Ottawa Parkway in ten minutes. I parked on a side street and set out on foot.

An entrance through a fence led me onto the bike path. The path ran parallel to the Ottawa River through the woods. I started calling Max's name, not certain which direction to turn. I thought I heard a noise coming from deeper in the bushes and yelled again. A few moments later, the bushes parted and Max stepped onto the path.

I blinked. "Where are your clothes?" I asked.

Max looked down at his bare feet. Only a pair of boxer shorts kept him from being completely naked. He was so skinny, his collar bones jutted out. I could count his ribs.

"I was robbed. They took my clothes and sleeping bag." His voice trembled. "They even took my ball cap." He sucked in a lungful of air and let it out slowly. "I'm sorry."

"You aren't the one who should apologize. You've done nothing wrong. Do you know who did this to you?"

He shook his head without looking up.

Anger made me breathe deeply to steady myself. There was no point getting upset. I had to think of how to help him.

My voice was determined, as if I was finding strength for both of us. "I have a blanket in my back seat. I'm going to pull my car up closer and you can wrap the blanket around yourself and climb in. Then, I'm driving to one of the outdoor shops to buy you some pants and a shirt while you wait in the car."

His voice was small. "Thanks, Anna."

"I'm happy to help."

I got the car and parked close enough for Max to jump in. He huddled under the blanket in the back seat and I drove first to a coffee shop. I got him a hot chocolate and a sandwich, then pulled into the parking lot of an outdoor clothing store. This time, I got him two pairs of everything, including a fall jacket and a ball cap the same colour as the one that was stolen.

He'd dozed off and I had to wake him when I got back to the car. I'd parked toward the back of the lot to give him some privacy. While he dressed, I stayed outside and leaned against the window to block anyone's view. I texted Jada.

Found our new office help.

When I got back in the car, I hesitated before turning the key. I turned backwards to look Max in the eyes. "Your aunt Sheila hired me to keep a watch over you," I said. "I'm a private investigator, not a social worker."

"I know."

"You know?"

"My friend Oscar told me. He followed you to your office."

What kind of PI was I? I'd been followed and hadn't even known. "Is Oscar living on the street too?" My voice sounded a little miffed.

"Yes. He likes to sleep in the men's shelter though."

"And you don't?"

"I like looking at the stars."

"What if I offered you a job and a room to stay in overnight?"

"I dunno."

"It's not safe for you on the street, Max. And we could really use someone to answer the phone."

He turned his head and looked out the side window. "What if I'm not good enough?"

My heart ached for this poor, broken boy. I reached back and touched his arm. "You are good enough. I believe in you."

"I guess I can help you then. If you don't tell my parents where I am."

....

Jada took one look at Max and sized up the situation quickly. "Welcome to Storm Investigations," she said, crossing the room and firmly shaking his hand. "We're swamped and I can't tell you how happy I am to have you aboard."

"Max is going to need a few things," I said. "Why don't you talk to him about the workload and I'll go to the drugstore?"

"Perfect."

Jada got busy showing Max the computer accounting program and he smiled at something she said. I left with a sense of relief, knowing Jada would mother Max like she did her younger brother Henry.

Jimmy phoned as I was climbing the stairs to our office with a bag full of stuff for Max—toothpaste, toothbrush, soap, shampoo, shaving gear ... I'd tried to think of what a guy would need if he was starting from nothing. "Hey, Jimmy," I said, pausing on the stairs. "What have you got?"

"Door to door came up with zilch. None of the neighbours know the last names of the couple who were living with Wanda Miller. They said that Wanda wasn't as friendly as she used to be. She stayed inside her house this summer."

"A behaviour change usually means something is going on. What about the autopsy?"

"Coroner thinks she'd been dead three days when you found her. Blow to the head with an object killed her. The big news is that she took a large amount of money out of the bank the day she died. She made withdrawals for the same amount back in February and April."

"How much?"

"Nine thousand dollars each time. That equals twenty-seven thousand dollars if my math is right."

"Didn't her bank question the amounts?"

"No. They're going through the security video tapes now but she might have used a different branch for the withdrawals."

"She was killed for her money."

"Looking that way. They might not have meant to kill her, but it doesn't change the result." Jimmy paused. "What do you plan to do next?" he asked.

"I'm not sure. You seem to have done most of the legwork. I'll have to give this some thought."

"Let's stay in touch."

I signed off and opened the door to our office. Max was nowhere to be seen. Jada held a finger up to her mouth.

"Shh. He's sleeping in the small room."

I peeked in. Max was sound asleep on the couch we'd put in there for our rest breaks. He looked at peace under the blankets we kept for naps. I returned and sat across the desk from Jada.

"Sorry, partner," I said. "I didn't know what else to do."

Jada smiled. "No worries. I like the kid. I invited him to my place for the night but he said no. He's marching to his own drummer."

"I need to find out what's upset him so much that he'd rather live on the street than at home."

"He's going to sleep here on the couch overnight. It's all arranged. He'll have the coffee going before we arrive in the morning."

"Thanks, Jada."

"If it was Henry in trouble, I'd like to think you'd do the same for him."

"I'd do anything for Henry. You can bet your last dollar on that. And I'm growing to feel the same way about Max."

CHAPTER SIX

I thought about phoning Max's aunt Sheila to update her but didn't in the end. Until Max told me what was going on, I'd keep his location a secret, as I'd promised him.

Dad and Evan were putting four apple pies into the oven when I arrived home at six o'clock. Sammy was sitting at attention, keeping an eye out for falling crumbs.

"These pies are for the party on Saturday," said Evan. "I offered but Grandpa said definitely no taste-testing."

"Grandpa can be tough that way."

I sat down at the same time as Jimmy walked into the house. "Hope I didn't interrupt supper," he said, looking hopefully around the kitchen. "Is that apple pie I smell?"

"Would you like to stay for Chinese food?" Dad asked. "It should be here in a few minutes."

"Well, if you insist." Jimmy went into the fridge and took out three beers. He opened them and handed one to me and one to Dad before sitting down. Evan jumped onto Jimmy's knee and Jimmy pulled Evan against his chest in a tight hug.

"Anything new on the Wanda Miller case?" I asked, wondering if that's why he'd stopped by.

"We got some fingerprints from the scene and are looking for matches in our database," said Jimmy. "Fingers crossed, so to speak."

"You believe Tori and Bevan killed her?"

"I believe that's a real possibility. They were smart to have her withdraw under ten thousand dollars each time. An amount over ten thousand would have alerted the bank."

"I've been wondering where Wanda first met them," I said. "I'm going to check out the local churches and seniors centre."

"Good idea," agreed Jimmy. "I brought over copies of the first police reports. You can keep them if you don't tell Shaw."

"No chance of that happening."

The doorbell rang and Sammy and I scooted past Dad to the front door. "The meal is my treat," I said over Sammy's barking. Buying supper was the least I could do since Dad had insisted on preparing the food for Saturday's party. He'd taken on all the work and lifted the pressure off me. The only thing I had to do was show up.

··········

I got up early the next morning and went for a jog. The stretch of good weather was holding for another day. I'd found that staying in shape made me feel better. Running helped me to work off stress and gave me time to think. And being outside in the sunshine made me happy.

After completing my neighbourhood route, I showered and took a travel mug of coffee with me on the drive to the office. I wanted to catch Max in case he had second thoughts about working for us. He could very well decide in the morning light to return to the street.

I opened the door to our office, closed my eyes, and said a silent prayer for Max to still be inside. Sometimes, wishes do come true. Max was sitting at Jada's desk typing on the computer. The smell of freshly brewed coffee drew my eyes to the full pot on the shelf under the window. I said the only thing I could think of at that moment.

"Good morning, Max."

"Hey, Anna. I'm working on the billing. I hope that's okay."

"Okay? It's more than okay. It's wonderful."

I filled my coffee mug and poured a second cup for Max. "Cream and sugar?" I asked.

"That would be great."

His eyes were focused on the computer screen, his fingers racing across the keys. I set the mug of coffee on the desk within reach. "You've got good typing skills," I said, standing next to him.

"Thanks." A red blush worked up from his neck into his cheeks, but he kept working.

"I have a couple of calls to make and then how about I take you for breakfast?"

"You don't need to do that."

"I haven't eaten and could use the company. I can also fill you in on some research we need to do this morning."

He stopped typing and gave me a sideways grin. "You're the boss."

Twenty minutes later, we walked down Wellington Street to Fil's Diner. The day was heating up nicely—a September to enjoy before the cooler autumn days set in.

Fil's was full of locals eating breakfast but we snagged the last booth. I ordered a breakfast club and coaxed Max into choosing the Fil's Combo: one pancake, one French toast, scrambled eggs, bacon, sausage, hash browns, and toast.

It was time to ask Max why he was living on the street. I'd struggled with how to approach the subject. A direct question seemed like the only way I'd get any information out of him.

I finally settled on this innocent conversation starter. "Do you miss living at home?" I asked after the server had brought us two cups of coffee.

"Not really."

I stirred cream into my coffee. "Was something going on?" The question was loaded but I needed to ask it.

Max looked anywhere but at me. The red blush had crept up his neck again.

"Max," I said softly. "I'm on your side. Let me help you."

"I was the problem." He dropped his head and stared at his hands folded in his lap.

"Did somebody tell you that?"

"My family is better off without me. I know that now." He was close to tears and I bit back my next question. Luckily, our meals arrived and we got busy eating. I stole glances at his bowed head while I chewed and thought about my next steps in finding out what was really going on.

We finished our breakfast and returned to the office. Max and I spent the morning phoning churches and community groups in the Alta Vista area. We asked if Wanda Miller had been a member and if they knew Tori and Bevan. The names were unusual enough that I hoped someone would recognize them, even without their last names.

An Anglican church minister said Wanda had attended his church. But he hadn't seen her in months. He was dismayed and sad to hear of her murder. He didn't know any Tori or Bevan. I let Max know this information before dialling the next number on the list.

Jada walked into the office at one o'clock carrying a large pizza from Gino. The smell made my mouth water. Jada set the box on the desk in front of Max. She said, "Hi kids. Hope you're hungry."

Max and I both looked at the pizza box, then at each other. I smiled. "I think we could eat a few pieces."

Max grinned at me and nodded his agreement.

It felt at that moment as if Max was finding some happiness with us—as if we might be able to get his life back on track. But I knew that part of this belief was wishful thinking. I still had to figure out what or who had sent him down this painful path. I had to know if he was still a threat to himself—or to anybody else.

CHAPTER SEVEN

At 3:20, I drove through Westboro to Broadview Public School. Classes got out at 3:45 and I planned to speak with Sara Keane, Max's twelve-year-old sister. A Google search had brought up a photo of her in the local paper. She and two school friends had raised money for the food bank. They were in grade seven, according to the article.

I parked on a side street and found a spot on the sidewalk where I could watch both entrances. A noisy crowd of kids streamed out the doors and I scanned faces. The groups of kids started to thin and I thought I'd missed her. At last I spotted Sara walking alone, looking slightly older than in the photo. She'd cut her long hair to shoulder length but her glasses were the same. I walked toward her with a big smile on my face.

"Sara?"

She stopped walking and looked at me. "Do I know you?"

"I'm Anna, a friend of your brother Max."

"Do you know where he is? Is he okay?" She stepped closer. Her eager eyes zeroed in on my face.

"He's fine. I'm helping him with a job and a place to stay. Do you have a minute to talk?"

She looked around. "I guess. Let's go over there." She pointed to the playground and we started walking toward the swings.

"Do you know why Max left home?" I asked her.

"He was sad . . . he didn't like all the rules."

"Rules?"

"My stepdad, Lester, was always . . . well, he likes things done a certain way."

"Parents can expect a lot of their kids. Is he tough on you too?"

"No, not like he was for Max." She was quiet but I could see a struggle going on inside her.

"I like your brother. He doesn't seem to realize what a great person he is."

Her smile came and went. She bit her bottom lip. "Lester lost his patience with Max a lot. Once, I came home early from school and heard him tell Max that Mom regretted ever giving birth to such a useless loser."

"Did you tell your mother?"

"She and Max didn't always get along, either."

"What was the problem?"

"Mom said not to air our dirty laundry." Sara turned away from me and pushed one of the empty swings. "Max slit his wrists in the bathtub two months ago. We got him to the hospital in time but he was still sad when he came home. He left a week later. I had no idea where he went. My parents said that Max has mental problems and we're better off not having him at home. They're worried Max will hurt us."

"Do you believe that?"

"I don't know, but I miss him so much. Would you take me to see him, Anna?" Sara turned to face me and took a step closer. Her eyes were hopeful.

"I can't yet, but know that he's safe."

"Tomorrow? I could meet you here after school. I'm supposed to be in band so my parents won't expect me home until after five."

"I'll talk to Max first. If he wants to see you, I'll be here tomorrow at the same time."

"Tell him … tell him that nothing is the same with him gone."

· · · · · · · · · ·

Before I left the office, Jada told me that Henry was dropping by after school. They'd take Max somewhere in the 'hood for supper. Satisfied that Max was looked after, I continued on home to read over the file Jimmy had given me.

Dad and his lady friend Betty were in the kitchen baking cupcakes when I arrived. I could hear their laughter as soon as I stepped through the front door.

"There you are, dear," said Betty, giving me a hug as I entered the kitchen. She liked to liven up her hair and this time her tightly permed curls were a cotton candy pink. Her pale blue eyes sparkled behind oversized glasses.

"What are you two crazy kids up to now?" I asked.

"Getting that party off the ground," said Dad. "I recruited Betty because there's so much left to do."

Betty patted my shoulder. "Don't listen to him grumble. He's as happy as a dog with a bowlful of liver treats."

"You know I really, really appreciate all you're doing, Dad. I have some work to do but could help later."

"We've got everything under control," said Dad. "All I need is for you to call Cheri."

"Already done," I said. I pulled my phone out to call her as I walked down the hall.

CHAPTER EIGHT

I finished reading the file of police reports and sat for a minute, thinking. All of the people who'd been interviewed were listed, including the neighbours. Hal and Laurie, the older gentleman and his daughter that I'd met outside Wanda Miller's house, were on the list. But hadn't Laurie mentioned a caregiver staying with her father during the day? There should have been another name listed at their address. I'd drive over in the morning to check.

Dad and Betty were sitting outside enjoying the warm evening. I joined them and sat on the steps so I had a good view of the stars.

"I bought out an extra glass," said Dad. He poured me a drink of Scotch. The three of us toasted to the end of summer and new beginnings.

Evan and Sammy were with Jimmy and I missed their energy. Jimmy would drop them off in the morning, though, on his way to work. I hadn't been able to reach Cheri but had left a message on her voice mail.

Nick would be home from his movie shoot in two more sleeps. But I wasn't letting myself get excited yet. I still had a lot of work to do before then. Luckily, with everything going on with this case and Max, my mind was busy. I would give Nick my full attention when the time came.

· · · · · · · · · ·

The next morning, I put on my running clothes and set out on a route that took me to Wanda Miller's street. Clouds had drifted in overnight, hiding the sun from view. A cooler wind had replaced the warmth and I zipped up my nylon jacket.

The lights were on in Hal's house. I rang the doorbell and a woman opened the door. She was about five foot five and plump, dressed in a loose track suit, her long grey hair braided on top of her head. She looked to be in her early fifties.

"Can I help you?" she asked.

"My name is Anna Sweet and I'm friends with Gail Miller, Wanda's daughter."

The woman's smile turned into a frown. "Such a tragedy. And so disturbing to have that poor woman murdered right next door. Nowhere feels safe anymore. Please come in." She opened the door wider. For someone feeling unsafe, she was about to let a stranger into the house. I stepped inside before she rethought her invitation.

"You're Hal's caregiver," I said, following her into the kitchen.

"Yes, my name is Ivy Dodds. I've looked after Hal for nine months now."

We sat at the kitchen table and she poured us each a cup of coffee.

"Where is Hal?" I asked.

"Hal sleeps until ten o'clock. He's up half the night, mind you."

"Tough work for you and Laurie."

"He was a teacher and still is a kind man when his mind comes around. But yes, looking after him is becoming more difficult."

"Did you know the couple living next door with Wanda?" I asked and held my breath. She could set us on the track to finding them.

"Hal and Wanda were sweethearts at one time. Hal liked to go over to her house to visit so I met Bevan and Tori many times. I actually took her photo on my phone. Would you like to see it?"

Would I like to see it? "Could you send her photo to me?" I asked.

"Of course. Here," she said, handing me her phone. "Why don't you punch in your number and hit send?"

After I forwarded the photo to my own phone, I studied Tori's picture. She was short and slender with brown hair in a ponytail and colorful tattoos covering her right arm. "Did you ever find out her last name?" I asked.

"She told me once." Ivy thought for a moment. "It was some kind of side dish. Let me think ... Bean? No, that's not right." She took a sip of coffee and smiled. "I've got it! Her last name is Rice."

"That's great. What did you think of her?"

"She was ... pleasant. Did you know that Bevan grew up on a farm? I never learned his last name."

This woman was proving to be a goldmine of information. I chanced another question. "Do you know how Wanda met them?"

"Wanda told me. Let me think." Ivy's brow creased in lines as she tried to recall. "Oh yes, they met at the mall. Wanda was looking for someone to help her out and they got talking. Funny how strangers can make a connection."

"Where are Bevan and Tori now?"

"They left all of a sudden on Tuesday, just after lunch. I saw them get into a cab with their suitcases. I was surprised they didn't say goodbye." A look of horror crossed her face. "Do you think ... no, they left before the murder. Didn't they? Oh my goodness. I never for one moment thought they could have killed Wanda, but ..." Her voice trailed away.

"Time will tell," I said. I didn't add that they were the only suspects. I finished my coffee and stood to leave. "Thanks for sharing this information with me."

I sent Tori's photo and everything Ivy had told me in an email to Jimmy as I walked home. The police would find them quicker than I could.

CHAPTER NINE

Jada and Max weren't in the office when I arrived. I settled in at my desk with another cup of coffee and began updating my Wanda Miller file. I liked to keep detailed notes on every step of a case. Late morning, I got a text from Jimmy asking me to meet him for lunch at Whispers Pub. I accepted and kept working.

At eleven o'clock, steps pounded up the stairs. Jada and Max burst through the door.

"Max had his first lesson in tailing a mark," said Jada. "He's a natural."

The blush was back, creeping up Max's neck into his cheeks. But he looked happy. "I followed the woman and she had no idea," he said. "Your jobs are so sick."

Jada said, "By 'sick,' he means cool. I know that from living with a teenager." She saw the look on my face and added, "No worries, Anna. He was never in danger. It's an insurance fraud case."

"Well, thank goodness for that," I said.

Max sat at Jada's desk and started working on the computer. He looked so much happier than when I'd found him on the parkway. Jada came over and sat on the edge of my desk.

"Any progress on the Miller case?"

"Actually, yes. I gave Jimmy enough information to track down the couple who'd been living with Wanda. I'm meeting him for lunch. Hopefully, he has some good news."

"I got an email from your dad about Saturday."

"Yeah?"

"He said he's making the get-together a cocktail party for Betty before she goes to Florida for the winter. Wants us to dress up in more than jeans."

"Really? He hasn't told me yet."

"Well, be prepared to dust off a skirt."

I smiled. "I might be able to find something at the back of my closet." I checked the time. "Oops, gotta go. Jimmy's waiting for me." I stopped in front of Max on my way out the door. "What do you say about going to see your sister Sara when school gets out for the day?"

Max looked up and blinked. "You've seen her?"

"Yesterday. She misses you."

He thought for a moment. "Okay."

"Okay?"

"Yeah. I miss her too."

. . . .

Jimmy was waiting for me at a table for two with a view of the street. We both ordered the daily special: mushroom soup with a bacon, lettuce, and tomato sandwich and a beer to wash everything down. The server left and Jimmy leaned back in his chair and grinned at me.

"Something good?" I asked.

"We've located Tori Rice but not Bevan. She was staying at the YWCA downtown. Your photo combined with her name were key to finding her. She should be waiting for us in the interview room by the time we finish lunch. Interested in coming to the station to watch the master at work?"

"Yes, in spite of having to look at your swelled head."

"I thought you'd jump at the chance. As a thank you . . ." He waved his hand over the table.

"Lunch is on me?"

"Well, if you insist." He smiled as the server set down a beer in front of him.

We ate quickly and drove in separate cars over to the police station on Elgin Street. Jimmy signed me in and took me to a room. I could see Tori sitting on the other side of the glass, but she couldn't see me. A microphone would allow me to hear everything being said.

After a minute or so, Jimmy entered the room and sat next to a small table pushed against the wall. He was angled so that Tori sat directly across from him, no table between them.

I leaned into the glass to get a better look at her. She appeared small and nervous, huddled into her red hoodie. Her eyes kept darting around the room as if she was looking for an escape. Jimmy asked her if she'd like a drink of anything or a sandwich but she shook her head.

"Do you know why we brought you here?" he asked. His voice was friendly.

"Wanda?"

"Yes. You and Bevan were living with her."

"She wanted someone to help her."

"Where did you meet her?"

"At the mall. She was upset and I asked if she was okay. We got talking and I told her that Bevan and I were new in town, looking for work. She asked us to stay with her."

"Were you surprised by her invitation?"

"Yes, but she was so nice. We both came to like her a lot."

Jimmy was laying the groundwork. Lulling her into a false sense of security. He asked more questions that led to the heart of the matter. He tilted his head to one side and looked her in the eyes. "Why did you leave her house so suddenly?"

Tori lifted a hand to her mouth and began chewing on a fingernail. Her foot began tapping with nervous energy. "We saw ... we found ..." Tori's voice dropped to a whisper. "She was lying in so much blood."

"Are you saying that you found her?"

"She wasn't breathing but her eyes were open. We knew that we'd get blamed."

"Why did you know that?"

"Because Bevan had been arrested for shoplifting once. He has a record. We were scared."

"You didn't think to report that she was dead to the police?"

"No. We just ... we just wanted everything to go away. But I keep seeing her lying there on the floor and I feel sick."

"Where is Bevan now?"

"He took the bus home to Toronto. He said that he needed time to think."

"Money was missing from Wanda's account. Do you know anything about that?"

"I knew she was upset when we first met her. She said that she was lonely but I thought she was scared. We didn't take her money, if that's what you think."

"What was the date that you met her at the mall?"

"April 10. I know because we'd been in Ottawa a week. We were thinking about going back to Toronto because we couldn't find work here. She kind of saved us. I wish she was still alive. I miss her."

I thought about what I'd read in the police reports. Two of the withdrawals from Wanda's account happened before April 10. For the first time, I began to doubt that Tori and Bevan had killed Wanda.

By the glance Jimmy directed at the camera, I could see that he was feeling the same way. I knew he'd track down Bevan and question him too. But we had to widen the search and find out who had stolen Wanda's money. We had to consider other suspects.

CHAPTER TEN

I made it back to the office to pick up Max with barely enough time to make it to the school to meet Sara. If Max had second thoughts about seeing her, he didn't say anything. Still, I couldn't tell if he was happy about the trip to her school.

"Are you close to your aunt Sheila?" I asked.

Max buckled his seatbelt before looking at me. "Why?"

"She's the one who hired me to watch out for you."

He seemed to think this information over. "I like her. But I was closest to my grandfather."

"Past tense?"

"He died in January. Grandpa Keane was my mother's dad."

"And where is your dad? I know that Lester is your stepfather."

"My real dad died, too, when I was ten. Car accident."

"I'm sorry. That must have been difficult. I lost my mom at the same age."

"My turn to be sorry."

We were quiet after that, each back in our own memories. Losing a parent was tough. The memories were forever bittersweet. The longing to see them again was never far from the surface.

When we neared the school, Max said, "I texted Sara to bring me a few things out of my closet. She'll be waiting."

"You have a cell phone?" I asked, surprised.

He grinned. "I got a new phone when I started working for you. Jada lent me some money. She's the best."

"She is that."

I took a while to find a parking spot and we had to walk a few blocks to the school. Sara was waiting near the fence. She flung herself into Max's arms and they hugged. "You're really here," she said. They broke apart and she picked up a bag from the ground. "Here's your stuff."

I stayed back to give them some time alone. They were talking with their heads together and didn't see the woman running toward them. Her shoulder-length brown hair was laced with grey and her face was determined. She was wearing jeans and a sweatshirt with Snoopy on the front. She grabbed Max by the arm and spun him around. Sara put her hand over her mouth, a look of horror on her face. I leapt forward.

"What do you think you're doing?" I asked.

"This is my son. I want him to come home."

"No!" Max yelled. He backed away and I squeezed myself between him and his mother.

"Max, this has to end," she said. "We can get you the help you need. You can't be living on the street with all your ... problems."

Max darted away and started running down the street. His mother tried to go after him but I held onto her arm. "He doesn't want to go home," I said. I waited for her to stop pulling away from me before asking, "And my question is, why not?"

"He's mentally ill, can't you see that?" she asked. "We need to get him into a long-term care facility."

Sara had remained quiet and I couldn't tell what she was thinking. After the first look of horror, her face had gone blank. "Let's go home, Mom," she said quietly. "Max will be okay." She stared at me and her eyes begged for me to look after him.

"This isn't over," Max's mother said before turning away. Her words felt like a threat.

I watched them walk past the playground. They stayed a distance apart. After they went around the corner, I picked up the bag Sara had brought for Max and hiked back to my car. I had no answers but a lot of questions.

Max was sitting on the curb between my car and a minivan. He stood when he saw that I was alone. His hands were shaking. His entire body was vibrating. "It's getting worse," he said. "I need your help."

I stood quietly next to him until he calmed down and his eyes focused on mine. "How about you drive back to the office with me? I need to get organized for tomorrow. Then you're coming to my house for supper. Dad's cooking tonight and you don't want to miss that. We can work out a plan to get you where you want to be."

His breathing slowed. I watched him gain control of himself. "You don't think I'm crazy, do you Anna?"

"I *know* you aren't crazy. We're in this together, kid. I'm not going to let you down. I'll get you whatever help you need."

Max didn't say anything but his silence was enough to know that he was willing to give me a chance.

··········

Max and I were in my car after finishing up at work when Jimmy texted me. He wrote that Tori Rice had been released from the station with orders to stay in town. Bevan had been taken into the station in Toronto for questioning. I wanted to ask Tori a question that only occurred to me after the interview was over. I glanced at Max as I started the car. "We need to make a side trip." I eased into traffic, heading toward downtown.

The YWCA was a high-rise a street over from the Queensway, the major highway that ran through the city. I texted Jimmy when I parked and he sent Tori's room and phone numbers. I called her from the lobby and she said she'd be right down.

"She's still on the suspect list so we have to be careful," I said to Max.

"I understand."

Tori looked tired and nervous. We found a place to sit in the lobby. "How are you doing?" I asked her, after introducing Max as my assistant.

"I'm okay. You said that you were helping the police?"

"Yes. I watched your interview today and have another question to ask you." From other cases, I was well aware of all the scams being used on seniors to get their money. "Did you notice Wanda getting any odd mail or phone calls? Someone stopping by the house, perhaps?"

Tori thought for a moment. "I can't think of ... wait a minute. She was getting calls from a woman who said she was from a seniors chat line. But Wanda refused to speak with her."

"Did she say why?"

"Wanda told me that the woman had seemed friendly at first. Then Wanda said that she didn't want to talk about her."

"Any idea which chat line?"

"The number should be in Wanda's phone. The name that came up was Friends for Life Chat Line. Wanda said the woman's name was Olivia and to stop answering when her name or the chat line name came up."

"Did Wanda seem upset?"

"I thought so. She'd never answer the phone when we were there. She asked me to tell callers she was sleeping. She seemed upset so I did what she asked."

"Was there anyone else bothering her?"

"Not while we were living with her."

"Well, thanks for meeting us, Tori. Do you have another job yet?"

"I might have a serving job. I don't want to go back to Toronto." Tori reached her hand out to touch my arm. "Bevan and I would never have hurt Wanda. She wanted us to stay with her. She was one of the kindest women I've ever met. I still can't believe anybody would kill her."

CHAPTER ELEVEN

Dad accepted Max arriving for supper without any fuss. I'd sent him a text explaining the situation. "Grab a seat and get ready for the best ribs you've ever eaten," Dad said to Max when he walked into the kitchen. Dad had been in the armed forces and gave orders rather than displays of affection.

Evan and his beagle were staying overnight. Max relaxed as Evan chattered about school and Sammy circled the table, on patrol for falling food.

"Max, you're sleeping in the spare room," Dad said. "No need to drive downtown at this hour of the night."

Max didn't argue and I caught him smiling at Dad when he wasn't looking.

"You've passed the test," I said to Max after dinner, while Dad was busy with Evan. "He only barks out commands to people he likes."

"He reminds me of my grandfather. He was gruff, too, but a pussy cat underneath it all."

I left Dad, Max, and Evan setting up to play a board game and went into my office. I typed an email to Jimmy with everything I'd learned from my visit with Tori. I could keep digging into the seniors chat line myself. But Jimmy had the resources to do a thorough search, and we were partners on this file.

I sat back in my chair and thought about Max and his family. His mother believed he was unstable and perhaps a danger to himself. I was having trouble matching her worry with the young man I knew. But I'd been fooled by people before.

I set about doing some research. I started with Max's family. His mother was named Diane. She worked in reception at a car dealership and his stepfather, Lester, was a bartender. They owned a townhouse in the east end of the city.

I looked at the house on Google Earth. The neighbourhood was run down and their town house was at the end of a row and without a yard. Neither parent had a police record. They appeared to be hard-working people without a lot of money.

Max's aunt Sheila worked in a spa and lived in an apartment in the west end. I was about to track down the grandfather's obituary when Dad called my name from the kitchen.

"You've worked late enough," he said when I came out into the hallway. "We're taking Sammy for a walk. You in?"

I looked at Max and Evan. Their faces were eager and excited and I didn't want to do anything to upset them. Work could wait an hour. "Sure, I'm in," I said.

"Yippee, Aunt Anna!" yelled Evan. He flung himself around my waist and gave me a hug. "This is turning into one of the best days ever."

"It's been a very good day," I agreed, smiling at Max and Dad.

Our walk ended with ice cream cones at the corner store. When we got home, Max went upstairs with Evan to read him a bedtime story, and Sammy loped up behind them. Dad and I sat at the kitchen table with a pot of tea.

"Max is a good kid," Dad said. "I don't see any issues with his mental health."

"I like him too, but he did try to kill himself."

"Depressed?"

"I'm not sure. I think he has low self-esteem." I thought for a moment. "His grandfather died and they were close. Maybe Max had a difficult time with his loss. I've got a bit more research to do but it'll wait until tomorrow."

"Evan and Sammy like Max," said Dad. "That tells me a lot."

I refilled our mugs from the teapot. "Can I do anything to help for Saturday, Dad?"

"No, I have everything under control. Is Nick still flying in on schedule?"

"He is. I pick him up at the airport tomorrow evening."

"As long as he's here for the party, I'll consider my work a success," said Dad. He flashed me a quick smile before picking up his tea.

··········

The next morning dawned bright and warm. I woke with happiness in my heart at the thought of seeing Nick. I started the day with a run through the neighbourhood and a shower. Max was waiting for me in the kitchen and we drove downtown together. On the way, I stopped at a drive-through to get coffee and breakfast sandwiches.

"Tell me more about your grandfather," I said while we waited for our order.

"Grandpa Keane was a good guy. Self-made."

"Self-made?"

Max turned to look at me. "You don't know who he is?"

"Nope, can't say that I do."

"He owned Keane's Cookies." Max sang the company's tagline: "Chewy, gooey bites of goodness. Keane's cookies make your day a little sweeter."

"Your grandfather was Amos Keane?"

"Yup. He's my mom and aunt Sheila's dad. But he wasn't the type to care about money or fame. In fact, he gave his fortune away to charity when he died."

I stared at him. His grandfather had made a ton of money baking cookies. I should know. The Caramel Crunch Blasters were a big part of my childhood. "Your grandfather didn't leave you anything?" I asked.

"No. In a way, I'm glad. I never wanted us to be about his money."

Our food arrived. I paid and started the car. Max began talking about the night before and how much fun he had with Evan and Dad. I could see that he didn't want to talk about his grandfather anymore so I let the subject drop. I couldn't stop wondering, though, why his grandfather hadn't left the family any money from his fortune. How much did a man have to dislike his own children to leave them nothing?

CHAPTER TWELVE

Jimmy was standing on the sidewalk in front of our office when Max and I arrived. "Got time for a ride, Sweet?" he asked.

"Sure, but let me open up the office for Max first. Jimmy, meet our newest office helper."

Jimmy said hello and shook Max's hand. He looked at me. His eyes were hopeful. "Does this mean Nick is finished working for you?"

"He doesn't need the work. Max does." I smiled. "But he and I aren't over."

Jimmy smiled back. "Now that's a real shame."

I got Max settled upstairs answering phone messages and rejoined Jimmy on the sidewalk. "Where are we going?" I asked.

"To visit Olivia Heard at the Friends for Life Chat Line. We tracked down an address on Arlington Street."

"That's not the nicest area of town." The street had a mix of aging apartments and attached houses.

Jada and Henry had moved away from it to escape the drug dealers. "I guess the seniors line donations aren't being used to pay for high rent, so that's a good sign."

"Yeah. You can talk to seniors by phone from anywhere, really."

Fifteen minutes later, we cruised past the address. The building was a two-storey brick double with no yard. The front door was propped open and a woman was carrying a load of stuff down the steps. A car was parked on the street with an open trunk. She crammed the box into the nearly full space and slammed the trunk shut.

"Well, well, well. What have we here?" asked Jimmy. He parked in front of the car and jumped out to stop the woman before she could make it back inside the house.

"Olivia Heard?" he called.

She stopped with one hand on the step rail and turned to look at him. Jimmy pulled out his police badge and her face drained of colour. I was out of the car and walked up next to him.

"What's this about?" she asked, turning to glance through the open door.

"You run the seniors chat line out of this residence?"

"No … well, once. The chat line is closed down."

"Why's that?"

"We're … I'm moving."

"Oh yeah? Where are you moving to?"

"Montreal. I'm starting a new job."

Jimmy looked through the open door. "Who's that inside?"

"My employee. She's—"

"Tell her to come out here."

Olivia glared at Jimmy. She took a few moments before she yelled at the woman inside. "Hey, this cop is asking to talk to you."

I was getting a bad feeling about these two. Jimmy had tensed beside me but he kept his voice low and even. "Are you the only ones who worked the seniors chat line?" he asked.

Olivia stuck out her chin. "What if we are? We only had enough people call to keep the two of us busy. That's why we shut the line down, if you must know."

"I'd like to see your business licence," said Jimmy.

"It's packed away," she said quickly. "Might take a while to find it. I can send a copy to you, if you want."

"Was Wanda Miller one of your clients?" I asked.

"No. We've never heard of a Wanda. Isn't that right, Ivy?"

"That's right." Ivy Dodds appeared at the top of the stairs. Her eyes were darting between Olivia, Jimmy and the car. Like a cornered rat looking for an escape route. Mid-dart, her eyes landed on me.

"I thought you were looking after Hal," I said, the puzzle pieces slotting into place.

Ivy licked her lips. "I quit. He's too hard to handle. You saw that."

"Perhaps you quit because you got all you could out of Wanda before you killed her."

Ivy screamed as if she was being attacked by angry bees. She flung herself down the stairs and landed on top of Jimmy, who went down hard. At the same time, Olivia turned and shoved me. I fell backwards onto the sidewalk. Luckily, my rear end took most of the impact and I didn't hit my head.

I took a moment to recover from the jolt and got slowly to my feet. I stumbled over to Jimmy and checked that he was breathing. He was lying on his back, out cold but alive. I leapt over him and chased after Ivy and Olivia.

Ivy was already in the car's passenger seat with her door shut. Olivia was in the driver's seat but her door was wide open. She was shoving the key into the ignition while reaching for the door handle. I lunged for her and slammed the full force of my body against her arm. I heard a crack and she screamed in pain. I shoved her hard against the seat and the car keys dropped to the floor. While our scuffle was going on, Ivy pushed her door open and fell out of the car onto the sidewalk.

I grabbed Olivia by her good arm and dragged her out of the car over to where Jimmy was still out cold. I pushed her to the ground while I got his handcuffs off his belt. Olivia didn't fight me when I cuffed the wrist of her good arm to the railing at the bottom of the steps. The other arm was hanging at an odd angle and she was whimpering in pain. But I had no time to worry about her now.

Ivy had a good half-block on me but I was younger and in better shape than she was. I could thank all those mornings I'd spent running off Dad's cooking. I caught up to her before she disappeared down one of the side streets and I tackled her to the ground. She rolled over and clawed at my face with her nails. I thumped her on the nose hard enough to make her screech. She grabbed onto her nose and I flipped her over like a fish and twisted one arm behind her back.

"Stop it! You're breaking my arm!" she screamed.

"Then stop fighting me."

She went limp and I eased off and yanked her to her feet, still keeping pressure on her arm. With my free hand, I pulled my phone out of my pocket and dialled 911. I gave the dispatcher all the information I had as I frog-marched Ivy back to the house.

"I still don't know why you killed Wanda Miller," I said. "But I can guess. She was tired of being threatened and robbed, and tried to stand up to you. You bashed her on the head to stop her from telling anybody before you and Olivia could leave town.

"I'm not admitting to anything," Ivy said. "But if things happened that way, I never meant to kill her."

"But you did. You took advantage of a kind, lonely old woman. She called what she believed to be a real chat line, for comfort, and you forced her to give you money. You are lower than low."

Olivia was right where I left her. She stopped yelling for help when I shoved Ivy onto the bottom step next to her. "Don't move, Ivy," I said. "Or this time I really will hurt you."

I crouched down next to Jimmy while keeping an eye on the two women. "Jimmy, wake up," I said into his ear. "Jimmy, can you hear me?"

His eyelids fluttered and a moan escaped his lips.

"You're going to be okay. The ambulance is on its way." I checked for bleeding and did what I could to make him comfortable. People were coming out of nearby buildings and gathering on the sidewalk. One girl had her cell phone out, taking a video. Jimmy was not going to be happy if she posted it online.

Sirens were coming closer and I breathed a sigh of relief. It looked like we'd brought Wanda's killers out into the open. But my main worry now was Jimmy. My fear eased when he reached up and grabbed my hand.

"Didn't see that one coming," he said.

I gently squeezed his hand. "Neither did I. Don't worry though. I'm taking care of them."

"Of that," Jimmy said, "I have no doubt."

CHAPTER THIRTEEN

I spent a few hours at the hospital. Jimmy had a sore head, a couple of cracked ribs, and lots of bruises. He insisted that he wasn't staying overnight. His mother arrived to take him home and I walked out of the hospital to the parking lot. My cell phone rang before I got into my car. I checked the number. *Jada*.

"Hey partner," I said. "What's going on?"

"They took Max."

"Pardon?"

"I couldn't stop them. His stepfather and two other men took him to the Royal Ottawa Hospital. They're having Max locked up."

"No!" My shock quickly turned to anger. "I'm going to find out what's going on."

Jada said, "I'm one step ahead of you. Come to the office and we'll handle this together."

"I'm on my way."

My heart was pounding and my hands were shaking. It took me three tries to get the car key into the ignition. I had to force myself to drive the speed limit. Getting into an accident would not help Max.

Jada was waiting on the sidewalk in front of our office when I arrived. I double-parked and she hopped into the passenger seat. As I eased the car back into traffic, she said, "I checked into the grandfather's estate like you asked. He left money to charity but he also left money to Max. He gets it when he turns eighteen."

"How much?"

"The lawyer wouldn't give a final number but she signalled I was getting close in my guesses around five million dollars."

I whistled. "What did the parents get?"

"Nothing. But the granddaughter, Sara, inherits a million when she turns eighteen."

"No wonder they want Max declared mentally unfit. They're trying to gain control of his money." I pulled over to the side of the road. "Let's switch places. I need to call Aunt Sheila and get her to meet us at the Royal Ottawa Hospital. Hopefully, she can convince the hospital staff to let Max go."

"What if she's in on the scheme?"

"Then Max is in even bigger trouble."

We got out of the car and I took the passenger seat while Jada took the wheel. I got hold of Sheila and she promised to meet us. I lowered my cell phone and thought for a moment. Jimmy wasn't in any shape to help us but his supervisor Johnny Shaw owed me. I had Shaw on speed dial and he answered on the first ring.

"You're having quite the eventful day, Sweet," he said after I told him why I called. "Yeah, I'll meet you at the Royal and I'll bring some back-up."

Jada found a spot in visitor parking and we ran across the grounds toward admissions. We fell through the front door. My eyes swept the room. Max was sitting in a chair with a burly man on either side of him. A third man, who I guessed to be his stepfather, Lester, was talking to a nurse. They all turned to look at us when Jada and I entered. I was shocked by the defeated slump to Max's shoulders and the vacant look in his eyes.

"We're here to take Max home," I said to the nurse.

"Who are you?"

"Storm Investigations. Max works for us."

Lester took a step toward me. He was a tall, bald man with bulging blue eyes. His hands formed into fists at his side. "We're waiting for the doctor to admit Max. He's a sick boy and he needs help."

"Not the Max we know," Jada said.

The door opened again and Sheila entered, followed by Shaw and an officer in uniform. The nurse looked from them to me. "I have no idea what's going on here," she said. "Max's stepfather arranged with their doctor to have Max admitted as an emergency case. He believes Max is going to harm himself again."

Sheila stepped forward. "I'm Max's aunt. He does not belong here. I want to take him home with me."

The nurse looked confused. "I have to admit that we don't normally admit someone without more consultation." She turned to Lester. "Dr. Paulson wanted to have a meeting with you and Max today to make an assessment. He's been delayed, as I told you earlier."

Lester pointed his finger at Max. "Just look at him. He's a mess. His mother and I are his guardians. He needs to be in the hospital."

"You've been doing your best to make Max fall apart," I said. "He's confused but he's not ill."

Max lifted his head and stared at me. I met his tired eyes. "It's okay, Anna," he said. "I'm not worth your time."

I took a step toward him. "Max, your grandfather left you a lot of money. You inherit a fortune when you turn eighteen. I believe your stepfather and mother are trying to take it from you."

Sheila stepped between Max and Lester. "Is this true? Are you and Diane really this horrible?"

"They told me that my grandfather left us nothing," said Max.

"He left you a lot of money," said Jada. "I spoke with the estate lawyer earlier today. He also left some money for Sara, but nothing for your parents."

Max started to rise from the chair. One of the men shoved him down by the shoulder.

Shaw pushed his way forward. "Don't touch him again or I'll have you for assault." He moved in front of Max. "Kid, do you want to be here?"

Max shook his head. "I'd like to go home with Anna." He looked at me. "If that's all right with you?"

"Of course," I said. "Evan would love to have more time with you, and my dad is always looking for new people to fatten up." I looked at Sheila. "Are you okay with that?"

She nodded. "Whatever Evan wants."

"Then I'd say we have a plan for now," said Shaw. "Max will stay with the Sweets while I look into this matter." He turned and all but growled at Lester.

"The way I see it, you are a whisker away from doing jail time. So don't do anything else that makes me regret not taking you in now."

CHAPTER FOURTEEN

Saturday was one of those perfect late-summer days that make you glad to be alive. I woke early to dusky twilight and the birds chirping in the trees. The night before, Nick and I had sat in the kitchen with Dad and Max talking until late. Nick left at midnight to get some sleep while I stayed at Dad's. I should have been tired in the morning, but I felt full of happy energy.

I dressed in my running clothes and slipped out the back door. The neighbourhood was barely awake. I only passed two people out with their dogs on my way back to our house. Dad was working in the kitchen and I joined him after a long, hot shower. I was surprised to see Cheri sitting at the table with a cup of coffee.

"You made it," I said, and realized how much I wanted her to be there.

She stood and we hugged for a long time. "Dad suggested we go to the spa for the morning to stay out of his hair," she said. "Grab a coffee and let's get going. Don't worry. They serve food."

"But Dad, you must need our help."

"As if," said Dad. "You two girls go catch up with each other and have some fun. My treat. I've got more help than I'll ever need. Max and Evan are here and Betty is on her way."

"Well, if you're sure." If it hadn't been a chance to spend time with Cheri, I would have said no. I was not a spa kind of girl.

"I've missed you," said Cheri, grabbing my hand in hers. We were sitting in white fluffy bathrobes with cups of tea and our feet soaking in warm, oiled water. Scented candles and soothing music took away all my troubles.

Maybe I've been a bit hasty in my judgment of the spa life.

"Evan's missed you," I said.

"He's happy with Dad and Jimmy and you. I'm not cut out to be a full-time mom." She let go of my hand. "I love him more than anything but he's better off living here. I know that in my heart."

"I'm not so sure."

We didn't talk about Evan again. Cheri knew how I felt and we'd only get angry with each other. This was not the day to be upset.

We drove back to the house early afternoon. I went up to my room to rest. I'd left my phone on the dresser and checked it for messages. Shaw had sent an update. Aunt Sheila had hired a lawyer to defend Max against his parents. They would not be putting him into a hospital anytime soon.

There was a second message from Jimmy. He was feeling better and would make it to the party. Olivia and Ivy were in custody. Olivia was singing like a canary, blaming Wanda's murder on Ivy. So far, Ivy had refused to say anything at all.

According to Olivia, Ivy met Wanda through her job next door looking after Hal. It was Ivy who suggested that Wanda would be a good client for the chat line. Olivia said that she and Wanda spoke several times on the phone, and she liked Wanda so much that she agreed to meet for tea.

Jimmy snorted into the receiver, and said, "I knew they targeted Wanda, but I let Olivia keep spinning her story."

The first time Wanda gave Olivia money, she claimed, it was out of kindness, for all the good work the chat line was doing. But Olivia admitted that she'd had to use more persuasion to get Wanda to make the second "donation." The third and last time Wanda withdrew money, Ivy offered to drive

Wanda to the bank. For no reason, Wanda attacked Ivy when they got back to her house, and Ivy had to defend herself. Unfortunately, Wanda hit her head and died.

Olivia had even shed a few tears when she said Wanda's death was nothing but a tragic accident, Jimmy added. He wasn't convinced they'd planned to let Wanda live, but he was sure his team would get to the truth, given time. Since the interview, he'd learned that Olivia and Ivy had been charged with conning seniors out of money in other cities. But they'd always managed to escape jail time.

I let out a sigh of relief. Their arrest wouldn't bring Wanda Miller back, but at least Gail would know what happened. She wouldn't spend the rest of her life wondering.

I lay down for an hour-long nap and fell asleep instantly. My phone alarm went off at two thirty. I got up, put on some make-up, and slipped into my white lace dress and high heels.

At five minutes to three, Dad knocked. I swung the door open and we stared at each other for a long moment. A lifetime of unspoken love passed between us. I reached up to straighten his tie. He patted my cheek. "I'm the proudest man alive," he said, his voice gruff. He handed me a diamond bracelet. "This was your mother's. She'd want you to wear it today and keep it as her gift."

"Oh, Dad. This is perfect."

He put my mother's bracelet on my wrist and we walked downstairs arm in arm. Dad had set up chairs outside and lined a pathway with vases of roses and baby's breath. Everyone I knew and loved watched my dad walk me up the aisle to where Nick stood waiting: Cheri and Evan. Betty, Max, Jada, and Henry. Johnny Shaw and Jimmy. Nick's father Gino, beaming in the front row with Nick's uncle and aunt and cousins beside him. Nick, Dad, and I had surprised them all—but this was how I wanted our day to be. A simple party with family and friends.

A friend of Nick's married us in the warmth of the late-summer afternoon. Nick and I promised to love each other through good times and bad until the end of our days. We'd be starting our life together with a trip to Italy for a month's honeymoon. Then we'd settle into the house Nick had bought two years ago, next door to Dad's.

We ate and drank and danced into the night. The warm, sunny day turned into a perfect evening and we stayed outdoors until the last guest went home at two a.m.

Everyone else trooped up to bed, but Nick and I didn't want the night to end. We took glasses of wine back outside and sat side by side on the steps looking up at the stars. I thought about how much my life had changed since my bartending days in the US and the phone call from Dad that brought me home. I'd been searching for happiness as far from Ottawa as I could get. But now I knew for sure that the happiness had been waiting for me right back where I started.

Nick kissed my fingers and turned sideways to look at me. "You seem far away," he said. "Is everything okay?"

I smiled into his beautiful dark eyes. "Mmm. More than okay. I was thinking about how happy I am. I'm not sure how my life got to this moment with you, but I'm awfully glad that it did."

He smiled back. "I feel the same way. I can't think of anyone I'd rather spend the rest of my life with than you, Anna Sweet."

I raised my glass and clinked it against his. "To us," I said, "and to all the wonderful adventures waiting for us around the corner. Between my PI business and your acting career, life will never be dull."

"To you, my love." Nick leaned forward and kissed me.

We lingered on the steps a while longer, staring up at the night sky. And I gave thanks upon the brightest star for all the people in my life. Nick and I were beginning a new chapter. I was ready to savour all the moments, to love him with all my heart, and to pack away every memory.

Because I knew at last that this town, with the people I loved more than life itself, was exactly where I belonged.

ABOUT THE AUTHOR

GRAHAM LAW

Brenda Chapman is a well-known mystery author. The Anna Sweet Mysteries are a popular series in adult literacy and English as a Second Language programs. *My Sister's Keeper* and *No Trace* were finalists for the Arthur Ellis Award. *The Hard Fall* and *No Trace* were nominated for the Golden Oak Award. A former teacher and senior communications advisor, Brenda makes her home in Ottawa.

ALSO BY BRENDA CHAPMAN

The Second Wife
Second Chances
In Winter's Grip
Cold Mourning
Butterfly Kills

Tumbled Graves
Shallow End
Bleeding Darkness
Turning Secrets

Anna Sweet Mysteries

My Sister's Keeper
The Hard Fall
To Keep a Secret
A Model Death
No Trace

Missing Her
Killer Heat
Too Close to Home

Jennifer Bannon Mystery Series

Running Scared
Hiding in Hawk's Creek
Where Trouble Leads
Trail of Secrets

You can visit Brenda's website at www.brendachapman.ca

Manufactured by Amazon.ca
Bolton, ON

33453106R00053